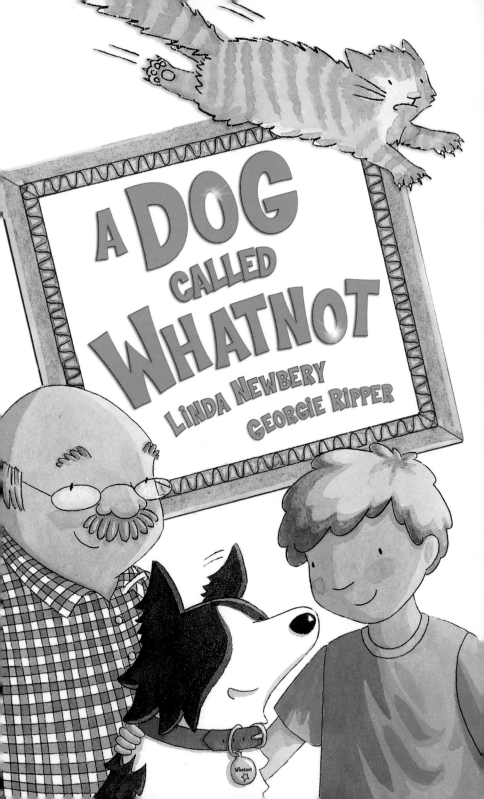

# A DOG CALLED WHATNOT

LINDA NEWBERY  GEORGIE RIPPER

**Crabtree Publishing Company**
www.crabtreebooks.com

PMB 16A, 350 Fifth Avenue,
Suite 3308,
New York, NY 10118

616 Welland Avenue,
St. Catharines, Ontario
Canada, L2M 5V6

For Olivia Hope Bursingham
L.N.

For Dad with love
G.R.

Cataloging-in-Publication data is available at the Library of Congress

Published by Crabtree Publishing in 2006
First published in 2005 by Egmont Books Ltd.
Text copyright © Linda Newbery 2005
Illustrations copyright © Georgie Ripper 2005
The Author and Illustrator have asserted their moral rights.
Paperback ISBN 0-7787-1094-7
Reinforced Hardcover Binding ISBN 0-7787-1078-5

1 2 3 4 5 6 7 8 9 0  Printed in Italy  5 4 3 2 1 0 9 8 7 6
All rights reserved. No part of this publication may be reproduced, stored in a retrieval system or
be transmitted in any form or by any means, electronic, mechanical, photocopying, recording, or
otherwise, without the prior written permission of Crabtree Publishing Company.

# Contents

Red Bananas

# LOST DOG

Whatnot arrived in Tim's life one summer afternoon.

Tim was in the park, playing cricket with Ajay, when he first saw the dog, watching from under the slide. It was a young collie, black and white, and smiley-faced. It watched carefully, as if wanting to join in. Tim aimed for the wicket – Ajay hit the ball into the bushes, and the dog ran after it. He scuffled and he rustled, then burst out again, carrying the ball in his mouth.

"Hey!" yelled Tim. "Give it back!"

The dog ran
twice around the
swings before
dropping the ball at
Tim's feet.

"He's better at fielding
than you are," Ajay
teased.

The dog waited
eagerly for Tim to
bowl again, and
bounded after Ajay's next
shot. His owner would soon whistle for him,
Tim thought, and take him away. But no one
came.

When it was time for home, Tim and Ajay
picked up their sweatshirts and turned for the
gates. The dog ran along with them.

"Is he lost?" Ajay wondered. "He's got no

collar. What should we do?"

"Better take him home," Tim said, knowing Grandpa would like that.

And not only Grandpa. *Tim* would like that. Tim had always wanted a dog of his own – a dog just like this one.

A dog with bright eyes and a smiley mouth.

A dog full of fun and energy.

A dog that would almost talk to him.

Come on, boy!

# LOUISA THE SNEEZER

Tim knew that he'd never be allowed to have
a dog of his own – however hard he promised
to look after it. Mom liked dogs. Louisa liked
dogs. Grandpa and Tim *loved* dogs – but there
was a big problem.

Louisa, Tim's sister, was allergic to animal
fur. Flora, her best friend, had two dogs and a
cat, and something about fur made Louisa
wheeze and sneeze. She'd snort and she'd
splutter and her eyes would go teary and
bleary and red. Louisa the Sneezer, Tim
called her. It was so bad that she couldn't go
inside Flora's house but had to wait at the

front door for Flora to come out.

If Tim wanted pets, Mom told him, he'd have to make do with a goldfish.

What use would that be?
A goldfish wouldn't be his *friend*.

This dog would. He
walked obediently
between Tim and Ajay,
pleased and eager. By
the time they reached
home, Tim never
wanted to part with him.

He could be:

A true and close friend.

A warm and furry friend.

A friend who'd always be ready to play
and explore.

A dog with no owner?

A boy with no dog?

Surely *something* could be worked out!

Heh, heh! Good boy.

# SILLY OLD WHATNOT

Grandpa and the dog liked each other at once. Grandpa found an old tennis ball, and hurled it down to the garden. The dog raced wildly after it, and brought it back in his mouth, snuffing and barking, smiling his eager-licky smile.

"You're a fine fellow," Grandpa told him, "a charming boy, a silly old whatnot!"

"I hate to spoil the fun," Mom said, "but he can't stay here."

"Don't take him inside, or I'll start sneezing." Louisa was clasping a tissue.

13

"You'll have to take him to the police station," said Mom. "His owner must be worried."

"But–" Grandpa began.

"But couldn't we–" Tim protested.

"To the police station," Mom said firmly. "Now. I'll find an old belt for a collar and leash."

"Oh, just when you've given him such a good name!" said Ajay.

"Name?"

"Whatnot. Silly old Whatnot, you called him. It's just right."

"*Whatnot! Whatnot!*" Tim tried. The dog cocked his ears and barked.

"Name or no name," Mom said, "he can't stay here."

14

Whatnot thought being on a leash was a new game. He bounced and leaped along the path, he pulled and he tugged, he crossed in front of Tim and back again, tripping him up.

"Come on," said Grandpa. "Let's get it over with. He must belong to someone."

"Perhaps they'll give us a reward!" said Ajay.

Tim didn't want a reward.

He wanted a dog.

He wanted *this* dog.

16

# LONG AND SHORT

In the Main Street, while they waited at the crosswalk, a big Range Rover pulled up. A row of faces looked out from inside: three humans, and five collie dogs.

A girl inside shouted, "That's our dog!" All five collies tried to push their noses through the window at the same time, while the woman driver stopped and got out.

Look!
There he is!

"Excuse me," she told Grandpa. "That's our dog you've got there. Did you find him running loose?"

Grandpa explained that they were on their way to the police station.

"We'll save you the trouble," said the woman. She opened the side door of the Range Rover. All the other dogs tried to run out, but the children held them back. "In, Wilmot!" she told Whatnot.

Whatnot pressed himself against Tim's legs.

"Wilmot?" said Grandpa. "We've been calling him Whatnot."

The woman laughed. "You weren't far off. In you get, Wilmot!" This time Whatnot obeyed, and the other dogs pushed

and huffed and
panted around him.
His owner unbuckled
the belt-collar and
handed it to
Grandpa.

Thanks for finding him!

"We lost him yesterday. He hates loud
noises. Someone fired an air-rifle at the park,
and he took off."

Hello, Wilmot!

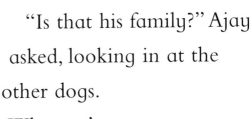

"Is that his family?" Ajay asked, looking in at the other dogs.

Whatnot's owner introduced them one by one. "This is his dad – Battling Braveheart of Bannockburn. And his

mom – Grangemouth Gliding Ghost. His brother – Westmoreland William the Bold. And his sisters, Shadowland Serena and Sutherland Sophie.

"I'm Fran Mann, and these two are Dan and Jan. Well, we're very grateful to you," she added, shaking hands with Grandpa.

HI!

"Bye-ee!" And she got back into the driver's seat and drove away. Dan and Jan waved through the window.

Whatnot looked wistful.

WOOF 1

1003 Poplar Street
Benton, KY 42025

*Goodbye, Whatnot,* Tim thought sadly.

"Fran Mann, Dan Mann and Jan Mann!" Ajay said. "They must give the dogs those long names to make up for having such short ones themselves. We never asked what Whatnot's — I mean Wilmot's — full name is."

"Whatnot," said Tim. "That's his name."

"Don't look so sad," Grandpa told him. "It's all for the best."

Tim scuffed his shoe. "He was such a nice dog. And we'll never see him again!"

I wanted him to be our dog.

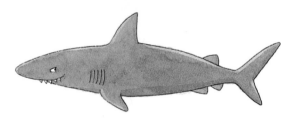

# NOT VERY BRAVE

But they did.

The next day, when Tim and Ajay were playing cricket in the park, there was Whatnot again – running in from the bushes, barking with delight.

Hey!

It's Whatnot!

He snatched up the ball in his mouth and
dashed off again.

"Whatnot!" Tim yelled. Whatnot knew his
name. He bounded up right away, dropped
the ball at Tim's feet, and dashed around and
around in wild leaps that made Tim dizzy.

"Maybe those Mannses are in the park,"
said Ajay, looking at the swings.

"Or maybe Whatnot got scared again,"

said Tim. "Or maybe he just likes us!"

They carried on bowling and batting, with Whatnot fielding. When it was time for home, Whatnot knew which way to go.

Good boy!

Ajay used his belt as a collar and leash. "This is like a replay of yesterday!"

"Except we know whose dog he is, now," Tim said.

Maybe *this* time, he thought, it would turn out differently!

Oh!

As they
crossed to
Park Parade,
a big Range Rover
drove up, and out got Fran Mann, on her
own this time.
"Thought I'd find him here!" she
said. "Come on, Wilmot." She
gave a little whistle. "Home.
A car alarm startled him this
time," she explained, while
Whatnot slunk into

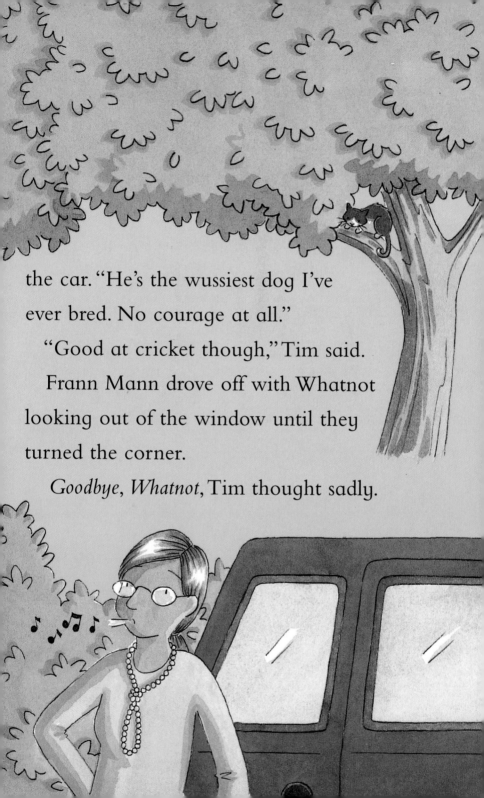

the car. "He's the wussiest dog I've ever bred. No courage at all."

"Good at cricket though," Tim said.

Frann Mann drove off with Whatnot looking out of the window until they turned the corner.

*Goodbye, Whatnot,* Tim thought sadly.

"*I'm* not always brave," he said to Ajay as they walked towards home.

Ajay thought for a moment. "You're not scared of dinosaurs. Or man-eating crocodiles."

"That's only because I don't meet them very often. I'm scared of – of swimming in the sea, for one thing. Of course, I know there won't be sharks or killer whales, but there just *might* be – especially when you start thinking about them. What I mean is, Whatnot's my kind of dog. My kind of dog exactly. But I don't suppose I'll ever see him again."

# WHATNOT AGAIN

"I really want a dog, Mom."

"Have you thought about what you'd like for your birthday?" Mom asked. "It's only two weeks away."

"I want a dog," Tim said.

Mom sighed. "Oh, Tim! We've been through this. You can't have a dog, because of Louisa's allergy."

We can't have a dog!

Huh!

"I'm not sure Louisa really *is* allergic to dogs, anyway," Tim grumbled. "I had dog hair all over my sweatshirt yesterday, and she didn't sneeze once."

"You think I'm making it up?" shouted Louisa. "You'd know all right if *your* eyes were red and itchy and you couldn't stop sneezing! Anyway, I *like* dogs!"

Tim went out.
He didn't even feel
like going to the
park today, but he
found himself going
that way, out of
habit. Ajay
couldn't play
cricket on his own.

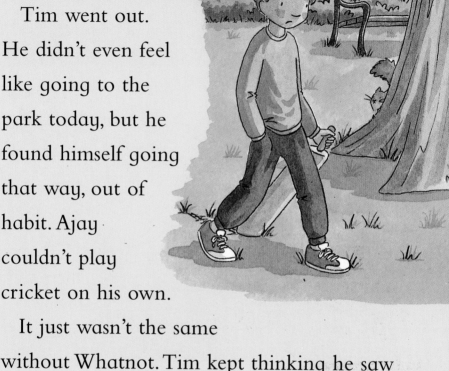

It just wasn't the same
without Whatnot. Tim kept thinking he saw
him out of the corner of his eye – but
once it was a paper bag, once a
duck that had waddled away
from the pond, and
**Munch!** once a
squirrel eating half
a sandwich.

Then, just as they turned for home, Tim saw Fran Mann and Grandpa outside the park, with Whatnot on a leash.

There's Whatnot!

The two boys hurried over. "He must have run off again!" panted Ajay.

Before they reached the park gates, Fran Mann got into her car and drove off, leaving Whatnot with Grandpa. As Tim approached, he saw Grandpa's face – beaming, grinning, glowing with delight.

"What's going on?" Tim asked.

"Why has she left Whatnot behind?"

Seeing him, Whatnot jumped up at his chest, panting and smiling.

"She's given him to us!" Grandpa said, with

the shiniest smile Tim had ever seen.

"But—" said Tim.

"He ran away again today," Grandpa said. "Brakes squealing frightened him. She's decided he's too much trouble. Whatnot's the only one without a special talent," he said.

He's ours!

"The others are sheepdogs, or show dogs or agility dogs. But Whatnot here's no good at anything. He likes us, and we like *him*, so she thought we could give him a home."

"But—" said Tim. Then he stopped Butting. The idea was too much to resist. "'Whatnot! Our dog!" He crouched to make sure Whatnot understood the good news.

"And she told me his real name," said Grandpa. "It's Wandering Wilmot the Brave."

"Wandering — yes. Brave — no," said Tim. "His name's Whatnot."

"Haven't you both forgotten something?" asked Ajay. "You won't be allowed to keep him. What about Louisa the Sneezer?"

# CATS AND DOGS

Tim was already beginning to feel sad. It would be *Goodbye, Whatnot*, yet again!

Grandpa looked sorry. "Well, we can't have young Louisa sneezing all day long. But I couldn't say no, could I? There must be some way around it."

"What – like Louisa moves out, and Whatnot moves in?" Tim said hopefully.

What about Louisa?

"We could build her a luxury kennel in the back yard."

"Louisa could wear a diving suit and an oxygen tank," suggested Ajay.

"We'll think of something," said Grandpa.

They were passing Flora's house. There on the front doorstep sat Louisa, with Flora, looking at a magazine. On the fence sat Marmite, Flora's tabby cat. Marmite arched her back and hissed at Whatnot – and then everything happened at once.

SLAM!

"**GOODBYE!**"

On the other side of the road, a delivery man closed his van door with a loud **SLAM**. Whatnot gave a loud **YELP**, turned on his tail, and set off at a mad gallop, dragging Grandpa behind him. "**WHOAH**!" yelled Grandpa. Marmite gave a piercing **YOWL**, and streaked towards the open front door of Flora's house. Flora uttered an ear-splitting **SHRIEK**, held out both arms and got tangled up with the cat. Louisa breathed in, her eyes wide.

Whoah!

YOWL!

40

**EEEEK!**

Tim waited

for it, covering his ears.

**"AA – CHOO!
AAAAAA – CHOO!
AAAAAAA – CHOOOO!"**

Marmite freed herself and
ran past into the hall.

Louisa *atish*ooed and *atish*ooed
and a**TISH**ooed. She blinked and bleared
through red teary eyes.

Tim looked down the road. Grandpa had
managed to stop Whatnot's wild dash, and
was leading him back.

Tim thought of the dog-hair-covered sweatshirt he'd left on the back of the sofa last night.

He thought of the dog hairs he'd carefully put on Louisa's pillow last night.

"**CATS!**" he shouted.

Ajay looked astonished. "What d'you mean, **cats**? There's only one cat, and it's just zoomed off like a ballistic missile!"

"I mean, Louisa's allergic to **cats**! Not dogs! It isn't Flora's **dogs** that set her off, it's Flora's **cat**!"

42

# JUST WHATNOT

Back at home, Mom had to be shown the
Sneeze Test. Louisa – after a bit of persuasion
from Tim - sat on the ground next to Whatnot

Hello, Whatnot.

and cuddled him, her face close to his fur. Not
a wheeze. Not a sneeze. Not a wink or a blink.

"So can we keep him?" Tim begged. "*Please!*"

Go on, Mom.

"Well," said Mom, rubbing her chin. "A dog needs a lot of looking after, you know! You'll have to take him for walks, even when it's raining, and take him to the vet for shots, and clean up his mess with a Poop-Scoop, and you've got to *love* him, always and always."

"I'll do all those things!" Tim promised.

"And so will I, when Tim's at school," added Grandpa.

"All right, then," said Mom. "We'll keep him."

I'll help!

Tim ran all the way down the yard and back again, leaping high in the air, with

Whatnot dashing in crazy circles around him.

"So,'" said Mom, when they were both tired out. "What would you like for your birthday?"

Tim thought hard. What more could he wish for now that his deepest, dearest, most desperate dream had come true?

"I'd like a cool new collar and leash, please," he said. "And a name tag, with Whatnot's name and address on it — just in case he runs off again."

"He's already got a name tag. Fran Mann gave it to me." Grandpa dug into his

pocket, and handed the tag to
Tim. "But it's got his old
name on it."

*Wandering Wilmot the
Brave*, Tim read.

"That's much too long,"
said Ajay.

"And too silly," said Tim.

"And only half true," added Ajay.

Tim handed the name tag back to

He's got a better name!

Grandpa. Whatnot wagged his tail and smiled.

"He's our dog now," said Tim. "And his name's Whatnot."

Just WHATNOT.

‑ated

W9-CLE-330

ler

Reading Level: _3.2_

Point Value: _.5_

MAY 2 2 2013

Marshall Co Public Library
@ Benton
1003 Poplar Street
Benton, KY 42025